DREAM BIG

Michael Jordan and the Pursuit of Excellence

Previously published as *Dream Big: Michael Jordan and the Pursuit of Olympic Gold*

DELORIS JORDAN

illustrated by BARRY ROOT

A Paula Wiseman Book
SIMON & SCHUSTER BOOKS FOR YOUNG READERS
New York   London   Toronto   Sydney   New Delhi

Schoolwork always came first, but whenever he could, Michael played, dreamed, and lived basketball.

Michael took his basketball everywhere. Every day when he got off the school bus, he would dribble his basketball home. But his love of his basketball made his mother tell him things like, "Michael, tables are for dining, not dribbling!"

Or "Michael, you may not play with your basketball in the house!"

And "Michael, put your ball down and concentrate on your homework!"

Every day after school Michael and his friends would play pickup games in Michael's backyard or at the boys' center downtown. They would see who could get twenty shots first. One afternoon Michael was way behind, not even up to ten. Michael's best friends, Reggie and David, were near twenty points each.

"Michael, you better catch up," David said. "Are you dreamin' again?"

Michael and his friends often talked about what they wanted to be when they grew up. Reggie wanted to be an astronaut, and David wanted to be a pilot. Michael dreamed of playing basketball, maybe even in the Olympics.

"David, do you think I'll make the team when we get to high school?"

"Michael, you love the game. The more you play, the better you'll be," David said. "It's like Coach tells us. You just need to work hard and keep practicing."

Michael was thinking about what David had said when he and the boys went over to his house to take some practice shots before dinner.

"Not so fast, boys. There will be no basketball until your homework is done. Every last page," Mrs. Jordan called.

"Moooooooom," Michael said.

"That's final. Now scoot."

"David and Reggie, see you later," Michael mumbled.

Michael knew his mom meant business. Schoolwork was important to her and came first. Basketball was fine, but only after homework was done, and done well.

Michael dragged himself to his room to work on Miss Gertrude's math homework.

At school that week all the talk was about the Olympics. The U.S. basketball team was playing in Germany and everyone was following it.

"I want to play basketball, not watch it on TV," Michael told his friends. Michael thought it would be so exciting to play for the U.S. Olympic team. He dreamed of it.

On Sunday, September 10, it rained and rained. Michael was stuck inside, so he watched the Olympics on TV with his brothers, Ronnie and Larry. The United States was playing basketball against Russia. It was the most exciting game Michael had ever seen, with a final score of 50–51, a loss for the United States.

After the game Michael walked into the kitchen as his mother was preparing dinner and announced, "I am going to be an Olympic champion."

"Oh, really," his mother replied with a smile on her face, not looking up from peeling the potatoes. "That's a long way off and you're just nine. You'll need to work hard starting today to make that happen." His mother wondered if Michael had any idea of all the effort it would take to even get to try out for the team. "Dreaming is good, but dreaming is for dreamers. It's one thing to want to play in the Olympics, Michael. It's another thing to do something about it," she told her young dreamer.

"Mom, I am a dreamer, but I am a winner, too."

"You better get busy, then. You'll be old enough to try out before you know it."

"Coach Herring, can I talk to you?" Coach had always given Michael a high five in the hallways, but still it had taken Michael weeks to get up the nerve to speak to him. "I really want to play on the U.S. Olympic team. What can I do to get there?"

"To start, you'll need to try out for the middle-school team. It's a lot of pressure and will be a lot of work, but nothing like the pressure in the Olympics. Can you handle it? I mean, deep down, can you handle it and do you really want it?"

"I promise to work my hardest and make it happen," Michael answered.

Michael was ready to play for his country in the Olympics and would do whatever he needed to do to get there.

"Well, son, with hard work anything is possible. Make sure you keep that promise to yourself."

The next day Michael's big brother, Larry, was off to Laney High School for a scrimmage. "I can't promise you any playing time, but why don't you come and sit on the bench and watch. Maybe you'll pick up some pointers and learn some new plays," his brother said.

Michael noticed that he was now up to Larry's shoulder. He had grown and so had his dream. It was time to do something about it.

Larry's team was leading by six points when Michael was called in.

Larry passed the ball to Michael, who passed it right back. Michael began to imagine himself on the Olympic team. He could see it and feel it. The ball was passed to Michael.

Michael had a mean long shot and he shot right over the head of the tallest boy on the other team. He sunk it!

"Mom, the final score was fourteen to ten. And three points were mine!"

"I guess you aren't just a dreamer, but a doer, Michael."

And Michael never gave up after that game. Not for a day. Even when he was cut in the tryouts for high school basketball, he just practiced harder and harder. Michael's big dream grew just like he did. In the 1984 Olympic games in Los Angeles, Michael Jordan became an Olympian for the U.S. basketball team and won his first gold medal. Somehow he knew when he was only nine that this is what would be. It all started during the pickup games on the blacktop with his friends. Michael never gave up. A giant step, no. A series of small steps, day after day after day, yes.

Michael's big dream came true. So dream big and work hard and your dream might come true too!

To Michael, who worked hard to keep the dream alive.
And to my eleven grandchildren: Follow your dreams and work hard
and they will become reality. Love you always, Grandma
—D. J.

For Kim
—B. R.

Previously published as *Dream Big: Michael Jordan and the Pursuit of Olympic Gold*

SIMON & SCHUSTER BOOKS FOR YOUNG READERS
An imprint of Simon & Schuster Children's Publishing Division
1230 Avenue of the Americas, New York, New York 10020
Text copyright © 2012 by Deloris Jordan
Illustrations copyright © 2012 by Barry Root
All rights reserved, including the right of reproduction in whole or in part in any form.
SIMON & SCHUSTER BOOKS FOR YOUNG READERS is a trademark of Simon & Schuster, Inc.
For information about special discounts for bulk purchases, please contact Simon & Schuster Special Sales
at 1-866-506-1949 or business@simonandschuster.com.
The Simon & Schuster Speakers Bureau can bring authors to your live event. For more information or to book an event,
contact the Simon & Schuster Speakers Bureau at 1-866-248-3049 or visit our website at www.simonspeakers.com.
Also available in a Simon & Schuster Books for Young Readers hardcover edition
Book design by Laurent Linn
The text for this book is set in Syntax LT Std.
The illustrations for this book are rendered in watercolor and gouache.
Manufactured in China
0216 SCP
First Simon & Schuster Books for Young Readers paperback edition May 2014
2 4 6 8 10 9 7 5 3
The Library of Congress has cataloged the hardcover edition as follows:
Jordan, Deloris.
Dream big : Michael Jordan and the pursuit of Olympic gold / Deloris Jordan ; illustrated by Barry Root. — 1st ed.
p. cm.
"A Paula Wiseman Book."
Summary: From the age of nine years Michael dreams of playing basketball for the United States in the Olympics,
and with hard work and his mother's encouragement, he realizes his dream.
ISBN 978-1-4424-1269-9 (hardcover : alk. paper)
ISBN 978-1-4424-3623-7 (eBook)
1. Jordan, Michael, 1963– —Childhood and youth—Juvenile fiction. [1. Jordan, Michael, 1963– —Childhood and youth—Fiction.
2. Basketball—Fiction.] I. Root, Barry, ill. II. Title.
PZ7.J7622Dr 2012   [E]—dc23   2011019441
ISBN 978-1-4424-1270-5 (pbk)